This book belongs to:

....

Mr. Happy

MR. MEN

and

Mr. Bump

Little Miss Splendid

LITTLE MISS

STORY TREASURY

Roger Hargreaves

A treasury of 10 magical fairy tales from
the Mr. Men and Little Miss Story Collection

EGMONT

We bring stories to life

MR.MEN **LITTLE MISS**

MR. MEN and LITTLE MISS™ © THOIP (a Chorion Company)

Mr. Men and Little Miss Story Treasury © 2011 THOIP (a Chorion company).
Printed and published under licence from Price Stern Sloan, Inc., Los Angeles.

First published in Great Britain 2011
by Egmont UK Limited
239 Kensington High Street
London W8 6SA

ISBN 978 1 4052 5881 4
47784/2

Printed in China

MR. MEN

and

LITTLE MISS

STORY TREASURY

Mr. Jelly

CONTENTS

MR. NOSEY

and the Beanstalk

Mr Nosey is one of those people who is curious about everything.

If he comes across a parcel he will start to wonder what's inside it.

And the more curious he becomes the more he has to know.

And even if it is addressed to someone else, Mr Nosey will not be able to stop himself opening it.

Just to have a look.

His curiosity always gets the better of him.

One day, Mr Nosey was out for a walk when he met a Wizard. The Wizard was holding a small bag.

Mr Nosey, being Mr Nosey, had to know what was inside the bag.

The Wizard told him that it was a bag full of magic beans.

Mr Nosey had to know what was magic about them.

"I will give you one bean," said the Wizard. "And if you take it home and plant it, you will find out. That is, if you're sure that you want to find out."

What a silly question. Of course Mr Nosey was sure he wanted to find out!

At home, Mr Nosey planted the bean in his garden. The next morning he could not believe his eyes.

There in the middle of his garden was a giant beanstalk that stretched up into the clouds.

As Mr Nosey admired the beanstalk a thought occured to him.

"What could be at the top of the beanstalk?"

The more he thought this thought, the more curious he became, and the more curious he became, the more he had to know.

So he began to climb the beanstalk.

He climbed …

... and he climbed ...

… and he climbed. Right up into the clouds. And when he reached the top he could not believe his eyes. (For the second time that day.) There in the clouds was a giant castle!

And then a thought occurred to him.

"Who might live in a castle in the clouds?"

And the thought grew into curiosity, and the curiosity got the better of him. So he set out across the clouds to the castle.

The giant castle had a giant door, and in the giant door there was a giant keyhole.

Mr Nosey cannot pass a keyhole and resist the urge to have a peek, and this time was no different.

Except that this time it was different because Mr Nosey could fit through the keyhole.

Once inside, it quickly became apparent that the 'who' who lived in the castle was a giant.

Now you or I would have sensibly left as fast as we could.

In fact, we would not have been there in the first place. But Mr Nosey, as you can guess, could not resist having a look around.

Mr Nosey went into the Giant's kitchen and in the corner were three small cupboards. Of course Mr Nosey had to know what was inside them.

He opened the first cupboard. Inside was a small bag, but before he could look inside the bag he heard a terrifying sound.

THUMP!

THUMP!

THUMP!

It was the thud of the Giant's heavy-booted footsteps somewhere in the castle, and they were getting closer.

Mr Nosey grabbed the bag, scrambled through the keyhole and slithered back down the beanstalk as fast as he could.

Safely back at home he discovered that the bag was full of gold coins!

That night he could not sleep. He lay in bed thinking about the other two cupboards.

"What could they contain?"

He just had to know.

Early the next morning back up the beanstalk went Mr Nosey, back through the keyhole and back to the second cupboard in the Giant's kitchen.

Inside it was a hen.

"That's curious," thought Mr Nosey to himself, not for the first time in this story!

He picked up the hen and there was a golden egg.

"A hen that lays golden eggs," murmured Mr Nosey. "I'll need to take this home for a closer look."

Just then Mr Nosey heard the heavy boots of the Giant coming down the stairs.

THUMP!

THUMP!

THUMP!

Mr Nosey tucked the hen under his arm and ran for his life.

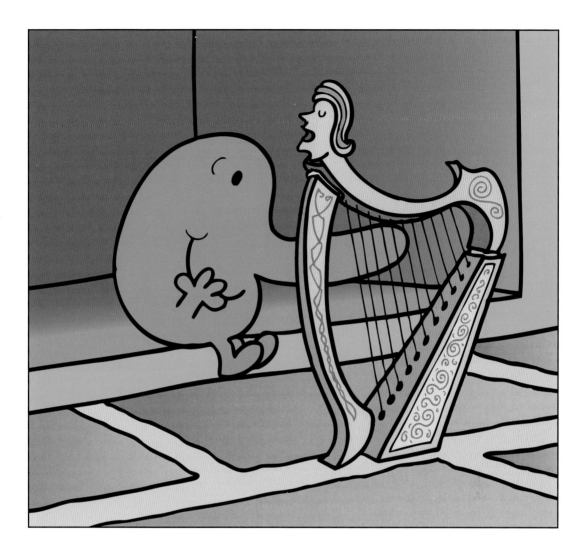

The hen fascinated Mr Nosey, but it did not stop him thinking about the third cupboard. He was terrified of the Giant, but his curiosity overcame his fear and so, the following morning, back to the Giant's kitchen he went.

He opened the third cupboard and in it was a golden harp.

A golden harp that was singing!

Mr Nosey sat and listened to the harp. He felt safe, knowing that he would be able to hear the Giant's loud boots coming.

But the Giant was wearing his slippers that morning, which is how he caught Mr Nosey.

"So you're the thief!" boomed the Giant. "I have a mind to grind your bones to make my bread!"

Mr Nosey's eyes nearly popped out of his head.

"But I won't," continued the Giant. "I prefer cornflakes for breakfast. Now, I know what to do with you. Since you are so interested in what is in my cupboards, you can clean them out for me."

And Mr Nosey did.

It took him three whole days.

Giant's cupboards are … well, giant.

"Now let that be a lesson to you," said the Giant.

And you'd think it would have been, but the very next day Mr Nosey came upon an empty house and the front door was open and on the kitchen table were three bowls of porridge …

... but that's another story.

LITTLE MISS STUBBORN

and the Unicorn

Little Miss Stubborn is, as you might imagine, the most stubborn person in the World.

She is as stubborn as a mule.

She is as stubborn as a herd of mules.

Once she has made her mind up about something, then there is no changing it.

For example, last week she decided to go on a picnic.

The weather forecast said it was going to rain.

All her friends said it was going to rain.

It was raining when she set off for her picnic.

And it rained on her picnic.

But she is so stubborn, she did not even take an umbrella with her.

The day after her soggy picnic, a very excited Little Miss Chatterbox telephoned.

"You'll never guess who I spoke to this morning," exclaimed Little Miss Chatterbox. "I was walking through the wood, the one down by the river, when I saw the most extraordinary sight! You'll never guess what it was. It was so exciting! I hardly know how to tell you. You just won't believe it, but it's true. I saw it with my own two eyes. It was incredible. I met a Unicorn!"

Little Miss Chatterbox can take rather a long time to say what she wants to say.

"Nonsense!" snorted Little Miss Stubborn. "Unicorns don't exist."

"But ..." began Little Miss Chatterbox.

"I don't believe you," interrupted Little Miss Stubborn and she hung up.

The next day, Little Miss Stubborn met Mr Bump.

A very excited Mr Bump.

"You'll never guess what I bumped into this morning. I bumped into a Unicorn!" he announced proudly.

"Nonsense," snapped Little Miss Stubborn. "Unicorns don't exist!"

"But ..." began Mr Bump.

"But nothing. I don't believe you," said Little Miss Stubborn and she walked away.

She passed by Little Miss Sunshine who was in her garden.

"If only you had been here half an hour earlier," called Little Miss Sunshine. "There was a Unicorn here in my garden and I rode on its back!"

"Nonsense!" exclaimed Little Miss Stubborn. "Unicorns don't exist!"

"But ..." began Little Miss Sunshine.

"No buts, I don't believe you!" interrupted Little Miss Stubborn.

And so it carried on.

It seemed that everyone had seen a Unicorn.

Mr Tickle had tickled a Unicorn.

Little Miss Greedy had fed a Unicorn.

And Mr Muddle declared that he had seen a unicycle.

Although, of course he meant to say a Unicorn.

And would Little Miss Stubborn believe any of her friends?

Of course not!

Not for a moment.

Little Miss Stubborn turned down the lane, through a gate into her garden.

And there, clear as day, helping itself to an apple from her apple tree, was a Unicorn.

"Hello," said the Unicorn. "I have been told that you do not believe in Unicorns."

"That's right," said Little Miss Stubborn. "Unicorns do not exist."

"So what am I?" asked the Unicorn.

"You," said Little Miss Stubborn, walking up to the Unicorn, "are a horse!"

With which, Little Miss Stubborn reached up and grabbed the horn on the Unicorn's head.

But to Little Miss Stubborn's great surprise, the horn was real.

The Unicorn really was a Unicorn.

"Well?" said the Unicorn. "What do you have to say now?"

Little Miss Stubborn screwed up her face and crossed her arms.

"I don't believe in Unicorns!" she said, and stamped her foot.

Stubborn to the very end.

MR. JELLY

and the Pirates

Mr Jelly is the most nervous person you will ever meet. The slightest thing will send him into a panic.

Even the sound of the wind in the trees will make him bolt behind the sofa, quivering and shaking in fear.

So as you can imagine, it takes Mr Jelly a long time to pluck up enough courage to go on holiday.

This year, Mr Jelly went to Seatown.

Mr Jelly longed to join everyone playing in the sea, but he was too frightened.

"Why don't you go for a swim?" suggested Mr Lazy.

"I ... I'm too scared," admitted Mr Jelly. "There might be nasty seaweed ...
or a crab ... or ... or a shark!"

"Well, why don't you go out in my dinghy?" replied Mr Lazy.

"I ... I ... might drift out to sea and never be found again," said Mr Jelly.

"No you won't," said Mr Lazy. "Not if I hold onto the rope."

Mr Jelly thought this over and decided to risk it.

After a while, Mr Jelly began to enjoy himself in the dinghy. But when he looked back, he discovered that he was a very long way from the beach.

Mr Lazy had fallen asleep and the rope had slipped through his fingers!

"Oh help! Oh help! A wave is going to turn over the boat and I'm going to be swallowed by a whale!" shrieked Mr Jelly. But he was too far away for anyone to hear him.

Before long the land disappeared and large, black storm clouds gathered on the horizon.

Thunder boomed and lightning crackled. The sea rose up in a great roaring mass that tossed the little dinghy from wave to wave.

Mr Jelly cowered in the bottom of the boat.

"Oh help! Oh help!" he shrieked. "I'm going to be struck by lightning, and burnt to a crisp, and tipped out of the boat and drowned!"

And then he fainted.

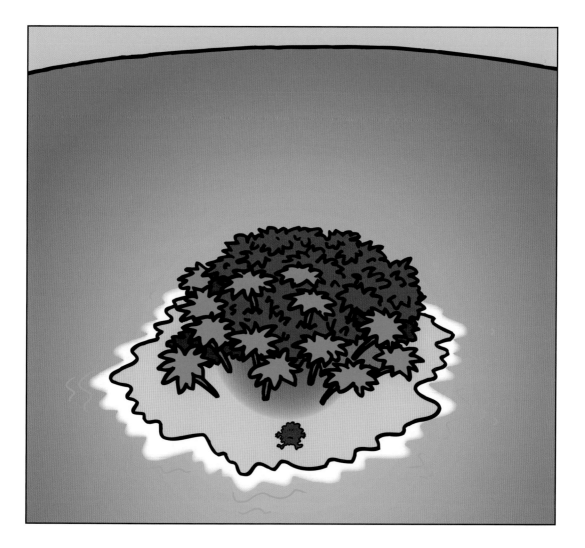

When he came to, he discovered that he had been washed up onto a tiny, deserted island.

Mr Jelly stared out at the vast expanse of sea.

"Oh help," he said in a very small voice, and then he fainted again.

Mr Jelly was woken by the sound of digging. He peered through the bushes at the side of the beach. What he saw filled him with terror …

Three swashbuckling, ruthless-looking pirates were digging up
a treasure chest!

Mr Jelly knew that he must not make a sound, but the more he tried not to
make a sound, the more he wobbled and trembled in fear. And the more
he wobbled and trembled, the more the bushes shook and rustled.

So, in a very short time, Mr Jelly was found and set, quivering, on the sand
in front of the pirates.

"Well, shiver my timbers, if he ain't just what we need," growled the pirate Captain. "A cabin boy!"

The three pirates and their new cabin boy rowed out to their ship, anchored in the bay.

Mr Jelly shook and trembled and quivered in terror.

The pirates, who prided themselves on their bravery, chuckled and laughed. They had never met anyone as nervous as Mr Jelly.

And over the following week, they came to realise just how nervous Mr Jelly really was.

On the first day, the first mate ordered Mr Jelly up into the rigging to set the sail.

"Oh help! Oh help!" shrieked Mr Jelly. "It's so high up and I'm going to have to climb and climb, and then I'll be even higher up, and I'll get dizzy, and I'll fall down into the sea and I'll be eaten by a shark!"

And then he fainted.

Luckily he had only climbed two rungs and the first mate caught him easily.

"I'd never thought of that," murmured the first mate to himself.

The next day, the quartermaster ordered Mr Jelly to sharpen the cutlasses on the grinding stone.

"Oh help! Oh help!" shrieked Mr Jelly. "I'll make the cutlass very sharp, and it will be so sharp that I will cut my finger, and then I'll bleed and bleed and ..."

And then he fainted.

"I'd never thought of that," mumbled the quartermaster to himself.

On the third day, the gunner ordered Mr Jelly to practise firing the cannon.

"Oh help! Oh help!" shrieked Mr Jelly. "I'll load the cannon, and then fire the cannon and the explosion will be so loud that I'll go deaf, and then I won't be able to hear anything, and then ..."

And then ... well, you know what happened then.

He fainted.

Again.

"I'd never thought of that," muttered the gunner to himself.

And so it continued all week.

Mr Jelly even fainted when the cook ordered him to light the stove in the galley because he was afraid he would set the ship on fire!

And a very strange thing happened during the week. Not only did the pirates discover how nervous Mr Jelly was, but they also began to find out how nervous they were, too.

The more Mr Jelly shrieked and fainted and quivered and quaked at what terrible accidents might happen, the more the pirates found themselves worrying. By the end of the week, the pirate Captain found himself with a crew who were too scared to do anything.

Even the ship's carpenter had downed tools because he was afraid he might get a splinter!

"This is hopeless!" roared the Captain. "How can we call ourselves pirates? That cabin boy has turned you all into scaredy cats. Mr Jelly must walk the plank!"

So, Mr Jelly was pushed out onto the plank.

"Oh help! Oh help!" shrieked Mr Jelly. "Don't make me walk the plank. I'll fall into the sea and then I'll have to swim for hours and hours and then I'll get weaker and weaker and then I'll drown!"

"That's horrible," said the first mate.

"Yeh, really nasty," agreed the quartermaster.

"We can't do that," said the gunner.

And the rest of the crew agreed.

"That's it!" cried the Captain. "I give up. Do what you want!"

And the crew did.

They sailed, very cautiously and very slowly, to Seatown, where they let Mr Jelly off.

Mr Jelly found Mr Lazy on the beach.

Fast asleep.

Mr Lazy yawned, stretched and opened an eye. "Hello," he said, sleepily. "Did you have fun? Sorry I fell asleep, but here you are safe and sound."

Mr Jelly began to wobble and quiver and shake.

Mr Jelly was very, very, very angry!

LITTLE MISS SHY

and the Fairy Godmother

Little Miss Shy is the shyest person that you will ever meet.

Except that you will probably never meet her because she never goes out.

So she didn't get excited when she received an invitation to Little Miss Splendid's Grand Ball. She got worried and flustered.

She wanted to go.
But she worried about all the people.
So, she would not go.
But she wanted to go.

Little Miss Shy was in a dilemma.

Plucking up all her courage, she rang Little Miss Sunshine for some advice.

"Do you know what I would do?" said Little Miss Sunshine. "I'd go out and buy a new pair of shoes. It always gives my confidence a boost!"

So Little Miss Shy followed her advice and went to the shoe shop.

"Please, I'd like to buy some new shoes," said Little Miss Shy in a very quiet voice.

"I CAN'T HEAR YOU!" boomed Little Miss Bossy, who worked in the shoe shop. **"SPEAK UP!"**

Little Miss Shy blushed.

"Oooh, look!" cried Little Miss Naughty. "She's turning pink!"

"Good gosh, you're right!" exclaimed Little Miss Bossy.

And she was right. Little Miss Shy was turning pinker and pinker.

"She looks like a strawberry blancmange!" giggled Little Miss Naughty, cruelly.

Little Miss Shy was, by this stage, pink from the top of her head to the tips of her toes. She burst into tears and ran out of the shop.

Poor Little Miss Shy.

She was so miserable she could not sleep.

She sat in front of the fire quietly crying to herself. "I will never go to the Ball," she sobbed.

"Oh yes you will," came a faraway reply.

Suddenly, a ball of light entered the room and as it grew brighter, a small, silver-haired woman appeared at its centre.

"Who are you?" asked Little Miss Shy.

"I am your Fairy Godmother," said the woman, kindly. "And you will go to the Ball."

"But I'm too shy," said Little Miss Shy.

"Not with the right pair of shoes," said the Fairy Godmother, who waved her magic wand.

Little Miss Shy's old bedroom slippers transformed into a pair of glass ballroom slippers.

The most beautiful shoes Little Miss Shy had ever set eyes on.

Then, the most amazing thing happened.

Little Miss Shy was suddenly filled with confidence. All her shyness disappeared!

"But, you must remember," warned the Fairy Godmother, "that on the last stroke of midnight on the night of the Ball, if you are still wearing the shoes, they will turn back into ordinary bedroom slippers."

The following evening, Little Miss Shy went to the Ball and she had the most wonderful evening of her life.

She danced all night long.

Everyone was dazzled by her beautiful glass slippers.

Little Miss Shy was so unlike her usual self that nobody recognised her.

Near the end of the Ball, Little Miss Splendid stood up and made an announcement.

"I have a surprise for you all. There is a prize for the best dancer at the Ball tonight, and I and my fellow judges have decided that this prize should be awarded to ... " she paused, "... the girl in the glass ballroom slippers!"

As Little Miss Splendid spoke, the bell in the clock tower rang the first stroke of midnight.

In a flash, Little Miss Shy remembered the Fairy Godmother's warning.

She couldn't go up and receive her prize without the glass slippers. Little Miss Shy could feel herself starting to blush. She panicked and fled from the ballroom.

As she ran, one of the glass slippers fell from her foot.

"Where is the girl in the glass ballroom slippers?" called Little Miss Splendid.

But nobody could find her.

She had disappeared.

All they could find was one glass slipper.

"I must have my winner!" cried Little Miss Splendid. "Search the land until you find her!"

So Little Miss Splendid's friends went out in search of a girl whose foot would fit the glass slipper. Everybody wanted to claim the prize, but nobody's foot would fit.

Little Miss Bossy and Little Miss Naughty tried on the slipper and of course it did not fit either of them.

"You should try Little Miss Shy," suggested Little Miss Naughty, slyly. "Let's go and watch her turn pink," she said to Little Miss Bossy.

"Oooh, you are naughty," giggled Little Miss Bossy.

So they all arrived at Little Miss Shy's house.

Poor Little Miss Shy. She did not know where to put herself.

And of course, she turned pink.

But not as pink as Little Miss Naughty and Little Miss Bossy when the glass slipper fitted Little Miss Shy's foot!

They were speechless!

"Little Miss Splendid will want to present your prize to you in person," said Mr Happy.

Little Miss Shy's prize was a pair of pink dancing shoes.

Her Fairy Godmother smiled down on her as Little Miss Splendid put the shoes on Little Miss Shy's feet.

They fitted perfectly.

And they matched Little Miss Shy perfectly.

Little Miss Shy was very proud and very pink!

MR. TICKLE

and the Dragon

Mr Tickle was having a very good day. Twenty-one people well and truly tickled. A very good day indeed.

But when he arrived home, he could not believe his eyes.

"I can't believe my eyes," he said to himself. "Somebody has burnt down my house!"

Mr Tickle's house was gone. All that was left was a smoking, charred pile at the end of his garden path.

There was more smoke rising from the end of the lane.

Mr Tickle set off to investigate.

The smoke was coming from Mr Funny's shoe car. Or rather, it had been his car, but all that remained was a burnt shoelace.

Mr Tickle could see another spiral of smoke in the distance.

This time it was Mr Clever's house, and very nearly Mr Clever by the look of him!

"I just got out in time," said Mr Clever. "There can only be one culprit. It must have been a ..."

But Mr Tickle did not wait to hear what it must have been. He had spotted the signs of another fire and was determined to follow the trail.

It was a long trail which led from Mr Chatterbox's burnt-out phone box to Farmer Field's burnt down barn, and on through wilder, bleaker land, up into the mountains. Soon it began to get dark, but Mr Tickle continued to climb higher and higher.

Darkness had fallen when he saw a bright light.

In the distance, there was a cave emitting a red glow.

Suddenly Mr Tickle did not feel very brave. Suddenly he wished he had stayed to hear what Mr Clever had to say.

Mr Tickle decided to wait there until the morning. He curled up under a bush and wrapped his arms around himself three times to keep warm.

Mr Tickle fell into a surprisingly deep sleep and the sun was up when he was woken by the rustling of the bush.

Mr Tickle opened an eye.

The bush rustled again.

"I know you're in there," rumbled a very deep voice. **"Show yourself!"**

Mr Tickle cautiously poked his head through the top of the bush and stood blinking in the bright sunlight. He was quite unprepared for the sight that met his eyes.

He was standing face to face with a Dragon!

A huge Dragon at that.

A huge Dragon with smoke curling from his nostrils.

Mr Tickle gulped.

"Hello," said Mr Tickle, in a tiny voice.

"I'm going to give you thirty seconds to give me a good reason why I shouldn't burn you to a crisp," bellowed the Dragon, **"and then I'm going to burn you to a crisp!"**

Mr Tickle gulped for the second time.

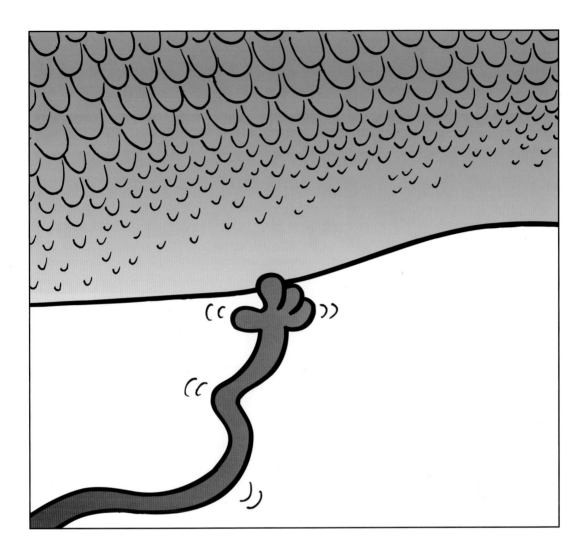

Mr Tickle needed to think fast. He realised his arms were hidden. Quick as a flash he sent one of his extraordinarily long arms snaking through the bushes and under the Dragon's belly.

Mr Tickle flexed his fingers and hoped beyond everything that dragons are ticklish.

The Dragon instantly crumbled into a giggling, laughing tangle on the ground.

"Ha! Ha! Ha!" roared the Dragon.
"Hee! Hee! Hee!" wheezed the Dragon.
"Ho! Ho! Ho!" boomed the Dragon.
"Stop it! Stop it!" he cried.

"I'll stop tickling if you promise to stop burning things," said Mr Tickle.

"Anything! I'll promise anything!" pleaded the Dragon.

Mr Tickle stopped tickling and looked the Dragon squarely in the eye.

"What you need to learn," said Mr Tickle, "is to put your fire breathing to good use. You should be using your extraordinary skills to make people happy. I'll show you."

The Dragon lay down on the ground and Mr Tickle hopped on his back. Then the Dragon shook out his great wings and took off, circling high over the mountains and swooping down to the distant valleys.

They flew lower and lower, passing over barns and cottages.

"Look!" cried Mr Tickle. "It's Little Miss Splendid's house. I have an idea for your first good deed!"

Mr Tickle and the Dragon stood beside Little Miss Splendid's swimming pool.

"It is too cold today to swim in Little Miss Splendid's pool," said Mr Tickle. "Do you think you could do anything about that?"

The Dragon thought for a moment.

Then he took a deep breath and breathed out through his nostrils. Flames licked across the surface of the swimming pool. In no time at all the pool was steaming.

Little Miss Splendid was delighted. Mr Tickle, the Dragon and Little Miss Splendid had a very enjoyable swim.

In fact, the Dragon had a very enjoyable day.

He melted the ice on Mr Bump's path, and Mr Bump couldn't have been happier, as most mornings he usually slipped up and bumped his head.

He warmed up Mr Forgetful's cup of tea which he had made at breakfast time and forgotten to drink. Mr Forgetful was delighted. He doesn't normally get to drink hot tea!

And Mr Greedy was very impressed when the Dragon cooked fifteen sausages all at once.

By the end of the day, the Dragon had a big glowing smile across his face.

"Do you know what?" he boomed, cheerfully. **"I feel really good!"**

Mr Tickle grinned and then he reached out his extraordinarily long arms …

… and tickled the Dragon!

"And now I do too!" he laughed.

LITTLE MISS SUNSHINE
and the Wicked Witch

Little Miss Sunshine was going for a walk. The weather was not very nice, but it takes a lot more than a bit of rain to dampen Little Miss Sunshine's spirits.

In the distance, she saw Little Miss Bossy approaching.

"I will be nice to Little Miss Bossy," thought Little Miss Sunshine, "so she won't boss me around."

However, as she got closer, the most incredible thing happened. There was a bright flash and Little Miss Bossy turned into a bat!

A blue, very squeaky, bossy sort of a bat.

"How extraordinary!" exclaimed Little Miss Sunshine, as she watched Little Miss Bossy flap her wings and fly away.

But almost as extraordinary was the cackling laugh Little Miss Sunshine thought she heard coming from the clouds above.

The next day was much nicer. The sun was out and there was not a cloud in sight. Little Miss Sunshine was happily walking along, wondering what had happened to Little Miss Bossy, when she saw Mr Rude walking towards her.

"I will be nice to Mr Rude," thought Little Miss Sunshine, "or he will be rude to me."

But at that moment there was a bright flash. And when Little Miss Sunshine reached where Mr Rude had been standing, she discovered that he had turned into a toad.

A red, very rude, angry looking toad.

And just like the day before, Little Miss Sunshine heard a cackling laugh. But this time it seemed to be coming from a nearby tree.

On her walk the following day, Little Miss Sunshine had nearly caught up with Little Miss Dotty when there was another blinding flash.

Little Miss Dotty had turned into a mouse!

A very confused, dotty, blond-haired mouse.

When Little Miss Sunshine heard the same laugh she had heard the two days before, she ducked behind a bush and waited to see if she could find out who it came from.

Suddenly, with a rustle of leaves, a Witch flew out from behind a tree.

A Wicked Witch on a broomstick!

A horrible hook-nosed, hairy, warty Wicked Witch, dressed in black.

Little Miss Sunshine felt very afraid, but she bravely decided to follow the Wicked Witch into Whispering Wood. It didn't take Little Miss Sunshine long to find the Wicked Witch's ramshackle cottage.

Nervously, Little Miss Sunshine crept up to the window and cautiously peered in.

The Wicked Witch was standing beside a large, black cauldron hanging over a fire. She was muttering to herself as she stirred revolting ingredients into the steaming pot. Little Miss Sunshine listened hard to hear what she was saying.

And this is what she heard:

"Hubble, bubble,
Toil and trouble,
Eye of newt and hair of hog,
Early tomorrow morning,
Turn Little Miss Sunshine into a dog!"

Little Miss Sunshine realised that she needed help and she needed it fast.

She tip-toed round to the front door where the Wicked Witch had left
her broomstick leaning against the wall. And without thinking whether she
could fly a broomstick or not, Little Miss Sunshine hopped on.

As it turned out she could. Just about. The broomstick rose up into the air
with a wobbly Little Miss Sunshine perched on top.

Little Miss Sunshine knew exactly who would be able to help – Little Miss
Magic. The broomstick took her to Little Miss Magic's house in no time at all.

"There's a Wicked Witch living in Whispering Wood," explained Little Miss Sunshine, breathlessly, when she arrived. She then told Little Miss Magic what she had seen and more importantly what she had heard.

"… and I'm going to be turned into a dog tomorrow morning!" she gasped.

"That's awful!" said Little Miss Magic. "But this is just the sort of problem that I like dealing with."

"I hoped you would say that," said Little Miss Sunshine.

"Now, I'll tell you what we are going to do …" continued Little Miss Magic.

The next day, at sunrise, Little Miss Sunshine and Little Miss Magic knocked at the Wicked Witch's door.

The Wicked Witch opened it and with a flash, her spell turned Little Miss Sunshine into a dog.

"Hee, hee, hee," cackled the Wicked Witch. "That worked like a dream."

It was then that Little Miss Magic turned the Wicked Witch into a cat!

A smelly, scraggy, black cat.

A smelly, scraggy, black cat that suddenly found herself looking up at a scary yellow dog.

The Wicked Witch cat let out a screech and fled.

And, barking noisily, the Little Miss Sunshine dog set off in pursuit and chased the Wicked Witch cat far away. So far away that she would never find her way back.

When Little Miss Sunshine returned, Little Miss Magic turned her back into her old self. She then turned Little Miss Bossy and Mr Rude back to normal too.

Little Miss Dotty took a lot longer to find as she was hidden in a mouse hole, and being dotty, she seemed not to have noticed that anything had happened.

"Are you feeling all right?" asked Little Miss Sunshine, after Little Miss Magic had said a few magic words.

"Why, of course I am," said Little Miss Dotty. "Why shouldn't I? Although," said Little Miss Dotty, twitching her nose, "I really fancy a nice piece of …"

"… cheese!"

MR. STRONG

and the Ogre

Mr Strong is the strongest person in the World. He is so strong he can balance an elephant on one finger.

But quite recently, it looked as though Mr Strong might have met his match.

One day, Mr Strong met Little Miss Tiny on his way home from the shops. Little Miss Tiny was crying.

"What ever is the matter?" asked Mr Strong.

Little Miss Tiny told him. She had been walking back to her house, carrying a lollipop over her shoulder when a huge, ugly Ogre had leapt out from behind a bush blocking her path.

"Gimme yer lollipop!" the Ogre had demanded.

Poor Little Miss Tiny had no choice, but to give the Ogre her lollipop.
Mr Strong was appalled.

"It is not far to my house," he said. "I'll make you a cup of tea and we can work out what is to be done."

With Little Miss Tiny sitting on his shoulder, Mr Strong continued on his way.

Just around the corner, they came upon Mr Rush sitting at the side of the road, looking very shaken.

"What ever is wrong?" asked Mr Strong.

Mr Rush explained. He had been driving along the road when an enormous, brute of an Ogre had loomed up in the middle of the lane.

"Gimme yer car!" the Ogre had demanded.

Poor Mr Rush had no choice but to hand over his car and watch helplessly as the Ogre drove away in it.

Mr Strong suggested that Mr Rush join him and Little Miss Tiny for tea.

They had walked the last half a mile to Mr Strong's house when they met a very upset and indignant Mr Uppity.

This time Mr Strong had a very good idea what the matter was.

Mr Uppity had been on his way to the bank to count his money when a huge, horrible Ogre had stepped out from behind a tree forcing Mr Uppity to stop.

"Gimme yer hat!" the Ogre had roared.

Poor Mr Uppity had no choice but to give the Ogre his hat. Which, not surprisingly, was far too small for the Ogre.

"I've heard enough!" announced Mr Strong. "Go inside and make yourselves some tea. I'm off to find this Ogre. I shan't be long."

Mr Strong had a pretty good idea where he might find the Ogre. Behind his garden, on the other side of the hill, there was a cave in the woods. Sure enough, this was where Mr Strong found the Ogre, lounging in the entrance to the cave, eating Little Miss Tiny's lollipop.

The only trouble was, there was not one Ogre, but three! They were brothers.

The Ogres slowly raised themself to their full, menacing height. Undaunted, Mr Strong marched up to the Ogres and introduced himself.

"Strong! Yer don't know the meaning of strong. Just look at yer!" mocked the biggest Ogre.

"If I prove I am stronger than the three of you, will you apologise to my friends and promise to stop bullying?" asked Mr Strong.

"Stronger than the three of us!" boomed the biggest Ogre. "Even my little brother is stronger than you!"

"Can he lift this?" asked Mr Strong, raising a large rock above his head.

"Easy peasy," said the smallest Ogre.

Mr Strong passed the largest rock to the smallest Ogre, but it was too heavy for him and the Ogre dropped it on his toe.

"OWWW!" he bellowed in pain.

"Out of the way, titch," snarled the middle Ogre, pushing the youngest Ogre out of his way. "I bet yer too weak to pick that up," he taunted, pointing at a huge slab of stone.

Mr Strong smiled and lifted it effortlessly.

"Your turn," said Mr Strong.

The middle Ogre tried with all his might to lift the slab of stone. He raised one end three inches off the ground before he dropped it, trapping his fingers underneath.

"OWWW!" roared the middle Ogre in pain.

"Let me 'ave a go!" thundered the third Ogre, who was possibly the least clever of the three, but by far the largest.

With an enormous effort, the biggest Ogre lifted the stone slab above his head.

"Beat that," he grunted through gritted teeth.

But then his knees began to wobble, his legs started to tremble, his arms buckled and the rock came down on his head, knocking him out cold!

Mr Strong picked up the biggest Ogre as if he weighed no more than
a feather and carried him, with the other two brothers following behind,
over the hill, back to his house where he set him down in front of his
three friends.

"Now we have got all that nonsense out of the way," said Mr Strong, "I think it is time you said sorry."

"We're sorry," mumbled the three Ogres in unison.

"We can't hear you," said Mr Strong.

"We're very sorry," said the Ogre brothers more clearly.

"Now that's done we can all have some tea," announced Mr Strong.

Which they did.

Although the Ogres did not stay long, as tea parties are not really their thing.

LITTLE MISS SPLENDID

SPLENDID

and the Princess

Little Miss Splendid, as her name suggests, is very splendid. She wears splendid hats and lives in a splendid house.

And how does Little Miss Splendid know she is so splendid?

She knows because she has a magic mirror that tells her so.

Each morning, Little Miss Splendid goes into her dressing room and stands in front of the mirror.

"Mirror, mirror, on the wall, who is the most splendid of all?" she asks.

"Little Miss Splendid is the most splendid of all," answers the mirror.

Next door to Little Miss Splendid's very splendid house is a castle, which has stood empty for many years.

One day, on her way to the shops, Little Miss Splendid noticed a sold sign on the castle gate.

"I wonder who has bought that?" she thought to herself.

The following day, she found out.

Little Miss Splendid was woken by a fanfare of trumpets. She looked out of the window to see three removal vans and a very splendid-looking coach and horses moving in procession up the castle drive.

A Princess had moved in next door!

At first, Little Miss Splendid was very excited. "Living next door to a Princess must make me even more splendid," she told herself.

She put on her most splendid hat and got ready to visit her new next-door neighbour. But, before she left, she stood before her magic mirror.

"Mirror, mirror, on the wall, who is the most splendid of all?" she asked.

"The Princess next door is the most splendid of all," answered the mirror.

Little Miss Splendid could not believe her ears. "But I'm the most splendid!"

"Not any longer," pointed out the mirror.

Little Miss Splendid watched the Princess for the rest of that week.

She looked at the Princess's splendid coach. She studied the Princess's splendid crown. And she noted the Princess's splendid robe.

Everywhere she went nobody noticed her any longer. All they talked about was the Princess and how splendid she looked.

Little Miss Splendid grew more and more jealous of the Princess.

The following week, Little Miss Splendid went shopping. She bought an incredibly ornate coach and four horses, a shimmering princess' hat and a splendidly long and flowing robe.

Little Miss Splendid was so pleased with her new purchases that she went straight into town to show them off. But no one took any notice of her.

"Good morning, Miss Splendid," said Mr Happy, without any comment on what she was wearing. "Did you hear that the Princess is coming into town later? I can't wait, it's so exciting!"

A very disappointed Little Miss Splendid went home and looked in her magic mirror.

"I do look splendid," she told herself, admiring her reflection.

But the mirror disagreed.

"The Princess next door is the most splendid of all," said the mirror. "And if I may say, you look a little ridiculous."

Little Miss Splendid was dismayed. But, what could she do?

The next morning, the answer came to her when she was reading the newspaper. The Princess had placed an advertisement for a coachman, a maid and a butler.

Little Miss Splendid smiled to herself.

A little later, she went round to see Mr Bump.

"There is a job going as the Princess's coachman," she told Mr Bump.
"It would be perfect for you."

"Really?" said Mr Bump, as he accidentally broke his window.

He hurried over to the castle to apply.

Then Little Miss Splendid went to see Little Miss Scatterbrain and suggested that she applied to be the Princess's maid.

"Really?" said Little Miss Scatterbrain, rushing off to the castle as fast as she could.

Lastly, Little Miss Splendid visited Mr Muddle who was very excited at the idea of being the Princess's butler – although he took a few wrong turns before he remembered how to get to the castle!

When Little Miss Splendid saw the Princess next, it was very obvious that her three friends had got the jobs.

Mr Bump had crashed the Princess's coach and wrecked it.

Little Miss Scatterbrain had ironed the Princess's robe and burnt a large hole in it.

And Mr Muddle had muddled up the crown and the bread. He had put the bread in the safe and the Princess's crown in the oven and melted it!

The Princess did not look in the least splendid.

Little Miss Splendid stood in front of her magic mirror.

"Mirror, mirror, on the wall, who is the most splendid of all?" she asked.

"Little Miss Splendid is the most splendid of all," came the reluctant reply.

"I knew I was the most splendid of all!" cried Little Miss Splendid.

"Although," continued the mirror …

... "I did hear that the Queen is coming to stay!"

MR. HAPPY

and the Wizard

Mr Happy goes to the Town Library every Saturday morning.

He went there last Saturday.

And he went there this Saturday.

He was looking along the shelves for a book to read when a very large and rather battered red volume caught his eye.

He pulled it out and looked at the spine.

It read, 'SPELL BOOK'.

He was about to return it to its place when a voice suddenly said, "Don't you dare! I've been stuck on that shelf for a week!"

Mr Happy dropped the book in surprise.

"Ow!" said the book, for it was the book that had spoken.

There was a face on the cover – nose, eyes, mouth, everything!

Mr Happy was too amazed to speak.

"Oooh," wheezed the book. "You get terribly cramped if you're wedged on a shelf for too long. Now then, what's your name?"

"Mr Happy," said Mr Happy, finding his voice at last.

"Hello, I'm a spell book," said the book. "I belong to a Wizard, but the silly, absent-minded fool left me here. Look! He even forgot his hat! When I was asleep someone tidied me away up on that shelf. I need a lift home. Will you help me?"

Mr Happy agreed, and wearing the Wizard's hat, with the spell book under his arm, he set off through the countryside.

Mr Happy felt just like a real Wizard!

Along the way they met Mr Forgetful who was standing beside a phone box muttering to himself.

"Do you have any spells in there that could help Mr Forgetful's memory?" Mr Happy asked the spell book.

"Of course," said the spell book, and opened on the right page.

Mr Happy read out the spell and watched Mr Forgetful.

"I remember!" cried Mr Forgetful. "I've got to ring Mr Chatterbox … and I forgot to lock my house … oh no, I forgot to turn off my bath … and I didn't post that letter … and I haven't bought any milk … and I must water the plants and …"

Mr Forgetful was frantically running around in circles by this point, worrying about all the things he had forgotten.

"Oh dear! Do you have any spells to make people forget things?" Mr Happy said to the book.

The spell book opened at a different page and as soon as Mr Happy said the spell, Mr Forgetful looked a lot happier.

Mr Happy and the spell book continued on their way and they heard
somebody talking to himself around a bend in the road.

"If I cross over now then I might get run over, but if I don't cross over then how
will I get to the other side? Oh dear, oh dear."

It was Mr Worry.

Mr Happy looked down at the spell book.

"Do you want to know if I have any spells to stop people worrying?" guessed
the spell book, and opened to the right page.

Mr Happy read out the spell.

"I don't care!" shouted Mr Worry, suddenly. "Hee! Hee! I'm worry free! I'll just close my eyes and step out into the …"

CRASH! He walked straight into Mr Bump on his bicycle.

"Maybe worrying is safer after all," said Mr Happy, and the spell book flicked over a couple of pages to the spell that would return Mr Worry to normal.

It was a very long walk to the Wizard's house. In the middle of the afternoon Mr Happy caught up with a hot and tired Mr Small.

"How about a spell for longer legs?" suggested Mr Happy.

"Coming right up," replied the spell book.

Mr Small's legs grew and grew.

He strode off down the road at a terrific pace, until he reached a tree and banged his head on a branch. The same thing happened on the second tree he came to. And on the trees all the way down the road.

BANG! OUCH!
BANG! OUCH!
BANG! OUCH!

Mr Happy winced.

"Shorter legs?" asked the spell book.

Mr Happy nodded.

By the evening they came to a wood.

"We're nearly there now," said the spell book happily.

Finally they reached a cottage in a clearing.

The Wizard opened the door. He was overjoyed.

"My spell book and my hat! I've been looking high and low for them for so long that I'd nearly given up hope! Thank you!"

He invited Mr Happy in for supper.

A Wizard's supper.

They ate Everything Pie.

The pie changed as they ate, so every mouthful tasted different!

After supper was finished and the washing-up spell had done its work, the Wizard turned to Mr Happy.

"There must be something I can do for you. Choose any spell you wish. Choose anything you want!"

Mr Happy smiled. "After seeing what spells can do, I think I'm happy as I am!" he laughed.

MR. BUMP

and the Knight

Mr Bump was thoroughly fed up. It did not seem to matter what he did, he always ended up getting bumped and bruised or scraped and scratched.

So, you can imagine how hard it was for him to find a job.

He had tried working at the baker's, but he had burnt his fingers on the bread oven.

OUCH!

He had tried being a bricklayer, but he had dropped a brick on his foot.

THUD!

OUCH!

He had even tried working at the pillow factory.

Who could hurt themselves in a pillow factory?

Mr Bump, of course!

He got a feather in his eye!

OUCH!

Every day it was bandage this and bandage that. Poor Mr Bump was very fed up.

Then one day, while Mr Bump was walking in the woods behind his house, he met someone who gave him a wonderful idea.

The perfect idea for a new job.

That someone was a Knight in shining armour, riding by on his horse.

Now, it was not the thought of the excitement and adventure of being a Knight that caught Mr Bump's imagination, nor was it the idea of the fame and fortune he might win. No, it was the Knight's solid, metal armour that caught his eye.

Shining armour that protected the Knight from bumps and bruises, scrapes and scratches.

"If I wore armour like that," thought Mr Bump to himself, "I would never need to worry about bumping myself again. I shall become a Knight."

Early the next morning, Mr Bump rushed to the blacksmith's to buy himself a suit of armour.

The blacksmith had to put the armour on very carefully to avoid Mr Bump's bruises, but when he had it on, Mr Bump looked at his reflection in the mirror and smiled.

Mr Bump then bought a book called 'Knights, All you need to know'.

"Now," said Mr Bump, opening the book, "what do Knights do?"

He read a whole chapter about jousting. Then he went out and bought a horse and a lance and went to a local jousting tournament.

However, Mr Bump quickly found out that he was not very good at jousting. Every time he sat on his horse he fell off.

CRASH!

The other Knights thought it was hilarious.

That evening, Mr Bump opened his book and read a chapter called
'Saving Damsels in Distress'.

The next day, he set off, on foot, to find a damsel in need of saving.

Fortunately, because it was very awkward walking in a suit of armour, Mr Bump found one near his house.

A damsel locked in a very tall tower.

"Will you save me, Sir Knight?" cried the Damsel.

"I will!" Mr Bump called back.

The Damsel let down a ladder woven from her long, fine hair.

But try as hard as he might, Mr Bump could not climb the ladder.

He kept falling off at every attempt.

BANG! CRASH! CLUNK!

Feeling rather sorry for himself, and even more sorry for the Damsel, Mr Bump trudged off home.

The next chapter in the book was entitled 'Slaying Dragons'.

"That's the one for me!" cried Mr Bump.

The following day, Mr Bump bought a sword and shield and went in search of a Dragon. There were not any nearby, so he caught the bus.

The Dragon was asleep on the top of a steep hill.

It took Mr Bump a lot of huffing and puffing to climb to the top.

When he finally reached the top, he raised his sword above his head to slay the Dragon, but the weight of the sword tipped Mr Bump off balance.

With a great CRASHING and CLATTERING of armour, he rolled all the way down the hill.

It was a very sad Mr Bump who got back home later that day.

He had to face the fact that he was not cut out to be a Knight.

He went up to his bedroom and took off his armour.

And then he noticed something quite remarkable.

When he glimpsed himself in the mirror, it was a very different Mr Bump looking back at him.

A Mr Bump without a bandage or a plaster in sight.

A Mr Bump without a bump or a bruise.

Mr Bump smiled.

And then he laughed …

… and then he fell over backwards and bumped his head on the bed!

Little Miss Shy

Mr. Jelly

Mr. Nosey

Little Miss Sunshine

Mr. Tickle

Little Miss Splendid

Mr. Strong

Little Miss Stubborn

Mr. Happy

Mr. Bump

Mr. Nosey

Little Miss Sunshine

Mr. Jelly

Little Miss Shy

Little Miss Splendid

Mr. Tickle

Mr. Strong

Mr. Bump

Mr. Happy